J
You S0-DTC-980

Book Donated By:

Clara Sulz
Director of Instruction (Retired)
School District 23 Central Okanagan

A MONSTER IN MY CEREAL

A MONSTER
IN MY CEREAL

by

Marie-Francine Hébert

Illustrated by Phillippe Germain

SECOND
STORY
Press

CANADIAN CATALOGUING IN PUBLICATION DATA

Hébert, Marie-Francine, 1943-
[Monstre dans les Cereales. English]
A Monster in my cereal

Translation of: Un monstre dans les cereales.
ISBN 0-929005-12-0

I. Germain, Philippe, 1942-   . II. Title:
Monstre dans les cereales. English. III. Title.

PS8565.E2M6513 1990   jC843'.54   C90-093894-3
PZ7.H43Mo 1990

Printed and Bound in Canada

Published by
SECOND STORY PRESS
585½ Bloor Street West
Toronto, Canada M6G 1K5

CHAPTER 1

A BAD MORNING

I WOKE UP feeling like a pair of dirty old socks. And all because of my little brother, Pip. Sometimes I just can't stand the way he'll do anything to get attention! That morning Mister Pip had to go to the hospital with Mom to have his tonsils out.

Which meant I'd have to spend two whole days of my vacation all alone with my father. He never looks after me for that long, and I knew he wouldn't have a clue. He'd want to watch some dumb sport on TV, and I wouldn't get to watch any of *my* shows. Not exactly fair!

To cheer me up, Mom had made French toast.

"Poppy darling, come and eat."

Poppy! It has to be the worst name in the world. So why did my parents choose it for me?

As soon as I entered the kitchen, Dad started his comedy routine. He actually thinks he's funny.

"Are you trying to look like the monster on the cereal box, Poppy?"

Great! I had just spent fifteen minutes

on my hair.

Mom tried to explain: "It's the new look, dear."

But he kept right on teasing: "It looks like the newest in haystacks to me! Ha ha ha!"

All he can do is make dumb jokes. He never takes anything seriously. Especially not me, his own daughter.

If you ask me, the monster on the cereal box looked very nice, like a huge white cat with fluffy fur. Its big eyes seemed to be staring at me.

To get back at my father I snapped: "I'd rather have a haystack on my head like the monster than stubbly whiskers on my face like you!"

Everyone burst out laughing.
Everyone except me, of course. It's hard to laugh when you really feel like crying.

Finally Mom and Pip got ready to leave. I had a big lump in my throat and tears in my eyes. But no one noticed. Everyone was too busy trying to comfort my little brother, who was scared he'd be scared of the operation. It was as if I didn't exist.

Just then, I could have sworn the monster winked at me.

CHAPTER 2

THE MONSTER

I KNOW, YOU'RE going to say it's impossible. The monster couldn't have winked at me. That's exactly what I told myself.

But I wanted to make double sure, without anyone else around.

So while my dad was in the bathroom shaving, I crept back into the kitchen for another peek.

The monster seemed as flat and still as any old picture on a cereal box. I told myself that's all there was to it.

I looked it straight in the eye. "Go on, let's see if you can wink again," I dared the monster, confident that it wouldn't move a muscle.

And then it winked at me again! I almost fainted when a tiny voice came out of the box: "Don't be afraid, Poppy."

Are you kidding? I've never been so terrified in all my life. It was like watching a horror movie on TV. But this time, I couldn't change the channel or turn off the TV.

It was really happening, in my very own house.

I opened my mouth to scream "Mom!" But nothing came out, not a single sound. And, my mother had already left.

Then, before my very eyes, the monster stretched its hand out of the box, as if it wanted to make friends with me. And it smiled the friendliest smile. My eyes nearly popped out of my head. I couldn't believe what I was seeing.

I timidly reached out toward the monster. Then all of a sudden I got the creeps. "Dad!" I yelped, backing away. I must have been white as a ghost.

But when my dad strolled into the kitchen, he had shaving cream on his nose: the old clown act. Normally I'd have found it funny, but this time I wasn't in the mood for games.

In panic I glanced at the table.
Wouldn't you know it, the monster was
once again a motionless picture on the cereal box.

There was no point trying to explain
anything to my dad. I knew he'd only make
fun of me and say my imagination was run-
ning wild.

"I'm going outside to play," I muttered, and ran out of the house as fast as Pip does when I threaten to bite his bum.

Then I wandered around the neighbourhood, thinking hard. I wandered for a long time. I'd never believed in monsters or ghosts or travelling through space or any of those weird things.

But now one of those weird things was waiting for me in my own kitchen.

And it was smiling at me and wanting to make friends.

Just the thought of it made my heart jump. A scared jump, but excited too.

I decided there was only one thing in the world I wanted: to be alone with that monster again. And this time I wouldn't run. No way!

CHAPTER 3
A TERRIBLE SHOCK

I RACED HOME and ran into the kitchen. Then I stopped dead. The cereal box was gone from the kitchen table!

"Dad! Where's the cereal box?"

"I threw it out, Poppy. It was empty."

I couldn't believe my ears.

"You threw out the cereal box with the monster on it?!"

"Yes," Dad replied, unconcerned.

What a disaster! I was stunned.

"Where? Where did you throw it?"

"In the garbage can."

"There's nothing in here!" I cried.

"Of course not, Poppy. I took the bag outside. Today's garbage day."

I couldn't believe it. Anger bubbled up inside me.

"You threw away my monster?!?"

"What's the matter, Poppy? Can't you do your hair without that picture? Ha ha ha!"

Believe me, he was the only one laughing.

My cheeks were burning and I was starting to see red. Probably smoke was coming out my ears.

"How could you?!"

"Poppy, I can't believe you care about that ridiculous monster."

Like a volcano, I blew my top.

"He's not ridiculous! You're the one who's ridiculous!"

Dad tried to calm me down.

"I didn't know you cared so much about the monster, Poppy. Try to understand."

But I was too hot to slow down. I was spitting fire.

Why don't YOU try to understand? Mom would never have done anything like that!"

Dad hates it when I compare him to Mom. Two little lines appeared on his forehead.

"Please, Poppy, calm down. I'm sorry. Don't cry. I'll buy you another box of cereal, just like that one."

But I could not be consoled.

"I don't want another one. I want that one."

And then, just to punish him, I added: "I'll never forgive you!"

Two more lines appeared on his forehead. We could have had a game of tic-tac-toe.

Just then, I heard the garbage truck
pulling up behind the house. It hadn't
passed by yet! There might still be time.

In a flash I was outside. The garbage
collector had picked up the bag and was
about to throw it into the truck. I yelled at
the top of my lungs.

"Wait! Don't throw that bag in!
There's something important inside!"

I rushed over to the truck and he
tossed me the bag. I ripped it open.
Fortunately, the cereal box was right on top.
The monster was safe and sound. Whew!

Clutching the box to my heart, I ran into my room and slammed the door behind me.

CHAPTER 4

CROSS MY HEART
AND HOPE TO DIE!

I COLLAPSED ON my bed, holding the cereal box tight.

I was trembling all over. This whole thing was Dad's fault. I'd always known he didn't really love me. Alright then, I hated him too!

The monster cocked its head to one side and gazed at me kindly. Even Mom never looks at me that tenderly.

"I'm right here, Poppy."

And just the way the monster said,

"Poppy," so gently, made it sound like the prettiest name in the world.

Then the monster jumped off the box and held out its arms to me. I said to myself: "This can't be true. I'm imagining things."

What would you have done if you were me? For a moment I didn't know what to do. Then I burst into tears and threw myself into the monster's arms.

"That's right, little Poppy. Have a good cry. You'll feel better."

Dad never knows what to do when I start to cry. But the monster gave me a big hug and held me close. Its soft white fur dried my tears.

Dad's face is so scratchy, but the monster's was as soft as a kitten.

It whispered sympathetically, "You can tell me all about it, Poppy."

I poured out my heart, and the monster listened as if I were the most important person in the world.

Not like Dad — he's so selfish. When he's around we can't watch our TV shows. Sometimes he even switches channels right in the middle of a program we're watching. Mom would never do that. (She doesn't like TV anyway.)

And Dad's wallet is always stuffed with money. He can buy whatever he wants. But when I ask him to buy something I want, he says it costs too much. Can you believe it?

And Pip and I are squished together in the little bedroom. We don't have any space to play. Mom and Dad have the big bedroom and they don't even like to play. Explain that!

The monster did not tell me to stop complaining. In fact, it was on my side. The monster couldn't believe what I have to put up with.

"Poor Poppy! This can't go on. We have to do something."

"I already tried talking to Dad, but he just turned it into a joke. Everyone laughs at me. There's nothing anyone can do."

"I can do something, Poppy."

"What?"

"I can do whatever you want."

I told myself the monster was just trying to make me feel better, so I blurted out the first thing that popped into my head: "Sometimes I wish I didn't even have a father!"

Then a very serious look came over the monster's face. It turned so quiet I almost felt nervous. I had to bite my lip to keep from giggling.

"I'll take care of everything, Poppy," the monster promised gravely. "Cross my heart and hope to die."

Then, with a wink, it turned back into a picture on the cereal box.

Exhausted, I fell asleep, cuddling the box close to me under the covers.

CHAPTER 5

THE SURPRISE OF MY LIFE

I HAD JUST opened my eyes the next morning when Dad knocked on the door.

"Poppy, it's me. I've brought you breakfast."

Well, usually I love breakfast in bed, but today it didn't seem like such a treat. I was wild to talk to the monster again. And I must admit I was a little ashamed of losing my temper the day before. Sometimes when I get started, it's not easy to stop.

Finally, but not very enthusiastically, I told my dad to come in. I could just imagine the breakfast he would have made for me. There'd be nothing yummy, because he never notices what I like.

Wow! How wrong could I be? There was a glass of freshly-squeezed orange juice, just the way I like it. And toast with jam in the middle and peanut butter around the edges, just the way I like it. I couldn't believe how good it smelled.

He sat down very gently on the bed, as if he was afraid to disturb the monster in me. And in the voice he saves for special

occasions, he said: "We should talk, Poppy."

I already knew what he would probably say. That he was doing the best he could. That it's not easy being a kid, and it's not easy being a dad either. But he loved me more than anything else in the world. And so on and so forth.

Then I was supposed to answer that I was sorry that I had been so mean, etcetera etcetera etcetera.

But I was just itching to see the monster again, so I suggested very sweetly, "Not right now, Daddy. Later, okay?"

"Okay, Poppy, if you say so."

I couldn't resist putting my arms around his neck and giving him a big hug. He had just shaved and smelled delicious. It was the strawberry-scented shaving cream I had given him for his birthday.

As he went out the door, he said in mock despair, "Sometimes I don't know what to do with you, Poppy."

"Neither do I sometimes, Dad."

And we both burst out laughing.

As soon as he was gone, I threw back the covers. And that's when I got the surprise of my life.

The monster was gone!

CHAPTER 6

A LIVING NIGHTMARE

I SEARCHED MY room from top to bottom, but found nothing. The monster had to be somewhere else in my house. I went into the living room.

Dad was just settling in to watch a sports show on television, but this time I didn't care. I had more important things on my mind.

"Did you lose something, pumpkin?"

I couldn't very well answer, "Yes, I've lost the monster on the cereal box." He

wouldn't understand. I could hardly understand it myself.

So I just told him I had lost my, uh, —
my hat.

"Your white hat, Poppy? It must be
around here. There's some white fuzz dan-
gling from the television set."

Aha! The monster must be close at
hand. I took a quick look around.

Then Dad opened his mouth. I was
expecting him to say, "If you'd put your
things away, you wouldn't have to spend so
much time looking for them." But instead,
Dad turned to me in astonishment.

"Poppy, there's nothing but cartoons
on every channel!"

Of course, I guessed right away who
must be responsible for that. But I answered
innocently, "Maybe it's a special day for
children."

"You've got to be kidding!"

"Well, sometimes there's nothing but

sports or election news all day long, Dad."

"Hmm! Well, I'll have to go out and buy a newspaper." And he went to his room to get his wallet.

Wow! This monster was amazing! Children's shows all day long! I whispered softly to the air:

"Monster, Monster ... where are you?"

Just then I felt a hand in my pocket. I whirled around and caught a flying glimpse of the monster, leaping out of sight.

"Hey, Monster, wait!"

I raced after the monster and bumped smack into Dad instead. He was coming back from the bedroom, with his wallet in his hand and a puzzled expression on his face.

I thought to myself, "Oh no! He must have seen the monster."

"Poppy, all my money is gone. Look, my wallet is empty."

"I didn't take it, Dad. Honest! I didn't touch anything."

I put my hands in my pockets, ready to turn them inside out and show him they were empty. But I stopped myself in the nick of time.

My pockets were bulging with something that felt strangely like money.

The monster had struck again!

Dad was shaking his head. "I don't believe for a minute that you could have stolen my money, Poppy. I must have dropped it somewhere."

He turned back to the bedroom to look for his money. I pretended to help, all the while searching high and low for my monster.

At the bedroom door we both stopped, frozen. Now it was Dad's turn to go white as a ghost. His eyes popped out of his head.

Imagine this! All of Pip's and my things were in my parents' big bedroom and all my parents' things were in our little bedroom. All the furniture, the clothes, our toys.

I had never seen Dad in such a state. He stood absolutely still, dumbfounded.

Then I knew I had to find the monster and tell it to stop! Things were getting scary.

But how could I tell Dad what was happening? He would never believe me. Dad has to have a clear explanation for everything, otherwise he goes crazy. (What would happen if children freaked out every time they didn't understand something? I ask you!)

It looked like the monster had taken me at my word. First, the TV. Then all Dad's money. Now the bedrooms. Next... What else had I told him?

That I wished I didn't even have a father!

Oh no! I only said that because I was angry. I never thought the monster would take me seriously.

Now I was really in trouble! I looked all around me, but there was no sign of the monster anywhere.

I *had* to warn Dad. But he'd only make fun of me, and the monster would surely make him disappear. Oh, I wished

Mom were here.

I had no choice.

So I ran to Dad's arms. Squeezing my eyes shut tight, I told him everything.

It's incredible. He didn't laugh. What's more, he actually believed me.

"I don't want you to disappear, Dad. I want the monster to disappear!"

Big tears started to run down my cheeks: I swear I wasn't even faking.

Dad thought and thought, all the while wiping away my tears.

"This monster will do whatever you want, is that right, Poppy?"

"Yes, but I didn't mean it when I said I wished I didn't have a father."

Then Dad came up with a brilliant idea. When he puts his mind to it, my dad can be amazing!

"Poppy, if the monster does whatever you tell it to do, then all you have to do now is ask the monster to disappear."

It was so obvious! Why hadn't I thought of that?

But I didn't just nicely ask the monster to please go away. At the top of my lungs I yelled: "Monster, go away!"

No sooner said than done. It was incredible.

I knew right away that the monster had disappeared because the television began to play sports again. Suddenly my pockets were empty, and when Dad opened his wallet it was full of money.

And the bedroom furniture was all back where it used to be.

Was I relieved! I felt like I'd squeezed out of a very tight bottle just before they put the lid on. All the same, part of my mind kept thinking that maybe there might have been a way I could have kept the cartoons, the money, the big bedroom ... and Dad. If only!

CHAPTER 7

CROSS MY HEART AGAIN

Y OU PROBABLY think I made this all up, or that it was only a dream. So do I!

My dad always says, children do let their imaginations run wild.

Finally, Mom and Pip came home. Hugs and kisses all round!

Dad and Mom carried the suitcases into their room.

"Pip was so brave at the hospital!" reported Mom. Blah blah blah.

Then Pip stole up to me and, raising

his big eyes to mine, confided: "When I got scared, I thought of you, Poppy. And I said to myself, even if Poppy were scared, she wouldn't act scared. So I didn't run away or anything."

And he put his little arms round my neck and gave me one of his famous sloppy kisses. I'm telling you, when my little brother wants to, he can be something else!!

All of a sudden, I heard Mom asking if some animal had been in the house.

"Look, there are long white hairs everywhere!" she exclaimed.

Pip was excited: he ran off to check it out. Dad smiled, looking straight at me. So I snuck up beside him and whispered: "Don't tell Mom. She wouldn't understand."

He winked at me. Then he promised: "Cross my heart and hope to die."

Just like the monster ... !

Marie-Francine Hébert

Marie-Francine Hebért started to write for children by chance and now can't do without it. This is probably because, like all children, she loves kisses, craziness, physical exercise, little birds, questions, bedtime stories, ice cream and still has so many things to learn, like how not to be afraid of the dark. She has been writing for many years — television scripts, plays, and children's books. *A Monster in My Cereal* is her first novel for children.

Philippe Germain

Since the age of ten, Philippe Germain has loved sculpture and painting. These days, among other things, he illustrates textbooks and books for young people.

His dynamic style infuses real life with a sense of colour, spontaneity and, always, plenty of humour.

When he's not drawing, he enjoys taking apart and putting back together jukeboxes and other things from his collection of 1950s objects.